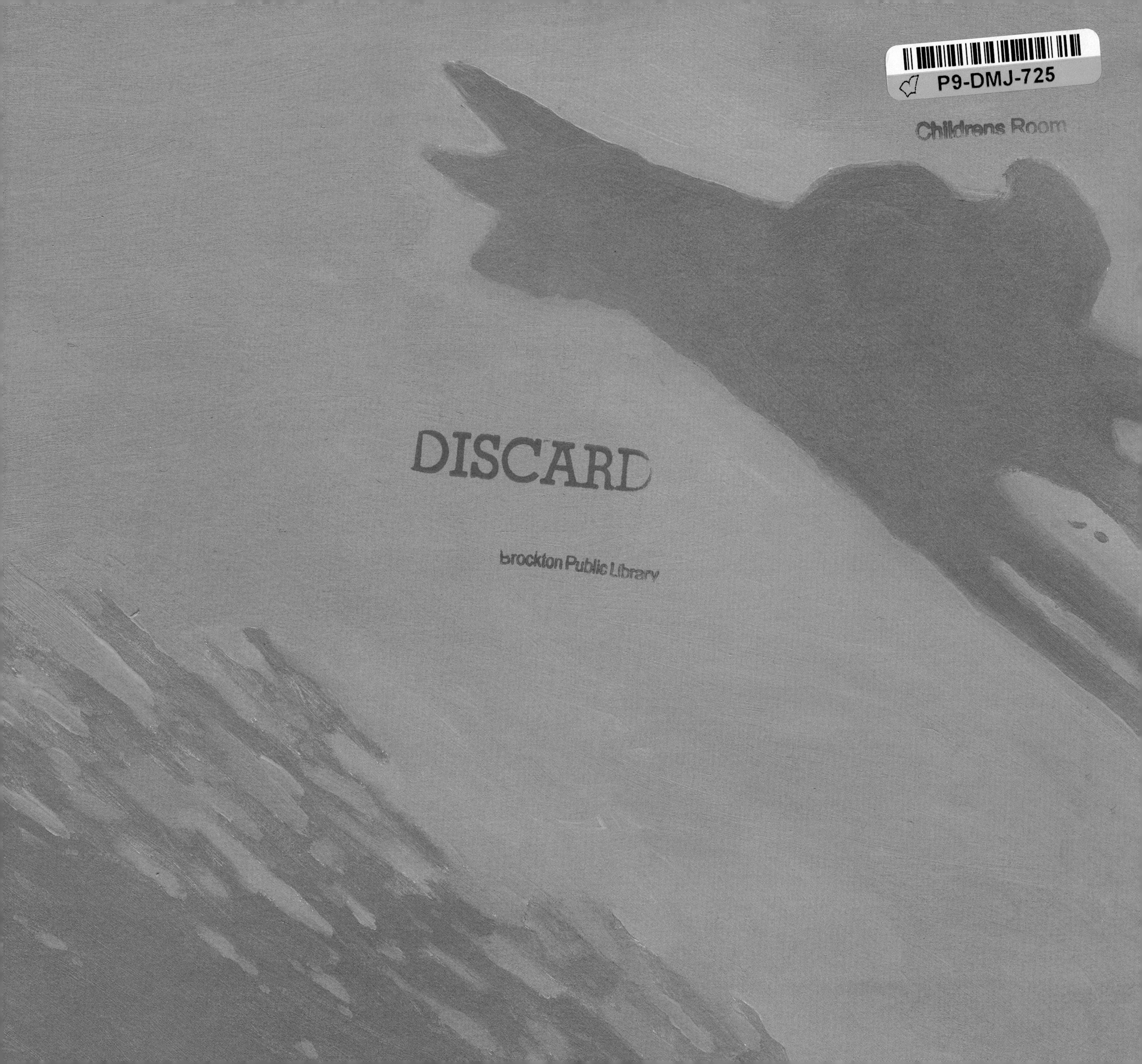

The
Blue House
Dog

To Molly, my blue house dog

—D. B.

For Henry

—A. G.

Ω

Published by
PEACHTREE PUBLISHERS
1700 Chattahoochee Avenue
Atlanta, Georgia 30318-2112

www.peachtree-online.com

Text © 2010 by Deborah Blumenthal
Illustration © 2010 by Adam Gustavson

Book design by Loraine M. Joyner
Composition by Melanie McMahon Ives

The illustrations were rendered in oil on prepared 100% rag paper; text is typeset in Goudy Infant and title is typeset in ITC Klepto.

Printed in Singapore
10 9 8 7 6 5 4 3 2 1
First Edition

Library of Congress Cataloging-in-Publication Data
Blumenthal, Deborah.
  The blue house dog / written by Deborah Blumenthal ; illustrated by Adam Gustavson.
    p. cm.
  Summary: A boy whose beloved dog has died, and a dog whose owner also died, find each other and slowly begin to trust one another.
  ISBN 978-1-56145-537-9 / 1-56145-537-7
  [1. Dogs—Fiction. 2. Grief—Fiction.] I. Gustavson, Adam, ill. II. Title.
  PZ7.B6267Blu 2010
  [E]—dc22
                                         2009040351

The Blue House Dog

Deborah Blumenthal

Illustrated by
Adam Gustavson

PEACHTREE
ATLANTA

I see him coming toward me,
and then I don't.

It's a hide-and-seek game
we play.

Sometimes he's there,
and sometimes he's not.

He gets by alone
on the street,
pawing at sacks of garbage
for scraps to eat.

Some people call him Bones
because he's so thin.
But nobody knows his real name.

He's just a stray dog,
people say,
and not a special one,
with his short scrappy fur
and tight muscles.
Half German shepherd,
half something else.

Only his eyes are special.
One is brown
and the other
sapphire blue.

He used to live with an old man
in a house painted ocean blue
on a street with daffodils
and tall trees as old as time.

The man had no one in his life
except the dog.
He took him for long walks
through the park
in our small town
just outside a skyscraper city.

But one day,
the old man stopped living.
He just sat in an armchair
in his house
for days
until the police
broke through the door.
The dog was crouched down
at his feet,
whimpering.

The police
must have scared him off
because he's been outside
ever since,
sleeping under a bush
with branches as rough as a brush.

I lay there once,
the grass hard on my face,
to see what it felt like
to be a dog without a home.

All day and night,
in sun and rain and snow,
he walks the streets now
with his smart pointy antenna ears up
and his head hanging down.

I whistle out
when I see him,
then run to the refrigerator
and pile a plate with
ham, franks,
anything I can find.

Bones leaps at the food.
When there's nothing left
he turns to go.

"Wait," I say,
reaching out.
But he's already gone.

I had a dog of my own once,
with black and white fur
and sad brown eyes.

Every night we curled up
together in my bed,
and in the darkness
of our blanket tent
I told him secrets.

His name was Teddy,
and he was my best friend
in the world.

But one day he got sick,
and no one knew why.

I have his picture
in my room.

When you lose someone
who's as close as your own skin,
the only place
you can find him again
is hidden
inside your memories.

One summer day,
Bones must have been thinking
more about food
than anything else.
He didn't see the car
pulling out.

"*Watch out!*" I screamed
as I raced towards him.
The car braked—
there was an awful screech.
I got there just in time.

When I tried to hold him,
he looked at me
unsure,
then slunk away.

Bones is just a stray dog,
people say,
and not a special one.
But he is to me.
Dogs find their way
inside you
and you want to keep them there.

There's a dogcatcher in town
who has his eye on Bones.
But Bones knows
when his black van
with the red letters
comes around.

One time
I saw his ears point straight up
when he saw it coming,
and he scrunched down
under a building,
waiting like a soldier
hiding from the enemy,
until it had gone.

On a gray day in winter,
they start to tear down
the blue house,
with Bones's old life
inside.

Now he'll have even less
than he had before.

The next time I see him,
I put a plate with roast beef
outside the basement door.
He licks the plate clean,
then looks at me
with his one brown eye
and his one blue eye.
I kneel down next to him
and whisper,
"Hey, boy, I'm Cody."

He lets me run my hand
lightly over his fur.
It's the same color as my hair.

With my other hand,
I open the door behind us.

Inside is the red striped blanket
that covers our worn green couch.
I put a biscuit on the blanket.

His ears go up and he dashes in,
grabs the biscuit,
then dashes out.

The next day,
I leave the door open
and put another biscuit there.
Then the day after,
again
and
again.

Each day,
he stays a little longer.

In my bedroom,
late at night,
I reach into my closet
under piles of books and toys
to where I buried a brown paper bag.

I dig it out
and slowly unwrap the dog dish.

I remember shopping for it,
looking in every store,
then,
finally,
picking just the right one
for my puppy.

It's fire-red
with smiling dog faces all over it.

After he died,
I didn't want to see it anymore.

Bones comes around every day now.
My home is becoming his new home,
so he needs a new name.
I look into his eyes
and say,
"*Blue*."

I take him for long walks
after school.
I don't need a leash.

He stays right next to me.

Whenever we pass the place
where Blue's old house used to be,
he makes a sound
so soft
that I'm not sure
if I heard it
or not.
It's a sad sound,
like a cry
from deep inside his heart.

But then we walk on
and go to the park.
I stop at a bench
and pull a small package
out of my pocket.

Blue cocks his head
and watches
as I tear open
the paper sprinkled with stars,
and unfold a blue bandana
that I tie around his neck.

The dogcatcher
doesn't come to our neighborhood
anymore.

There are no stray dogs
around here now.

Blue likes it that way,
and so do I.